Beliefs Across the River

Chronicles

of

the Mising Villages

SHIVA PRASAD MILI

Intentionally Left Blank

Published by

First Edition: 2023

ISBN: 979-88-913312-04

Printed and bound in India by Notion Press

Dedication

To all the tribal humanities, rich in lore and wisdom, who find solace in the embrace of legends. May you forever weave enchantment around the burdens of life and find respite in the magic of stories.

Acknowledgements

In the realm of storytelling, no tale stands alone. With heartfelt gratitude, I extend my appreciation to those who have journeyed with me through the pages of this book.

To my beloved family, especially my wife, Popy Pegu Mili, whose unwavering support and understanding have been my anchor and inspiration.

To the guiding light of my literary voyage, Prof. Mridul Bordoloi, your mentorship has infused my words with purpose and depth.

To the age-old men and women of Disangmukh, whose stories have echoed through generations and have now found a home within these pages.

And to all those who cherish the allure of folklore and the magic of tales, your appreciation fuels the fires of creativity.

May the echoes of these words resonate with you as they have with me.

Preface

As the author of this book, I find myself drawn into a realm of mysteries, a world where the threads of reality and superstition entwine. The inspiration for this narrative came from my conversations with old men and dear friends from the Mising (Miri) community, who passionately shared their encounters with the mysterious Baak, Dhanguli, Dangriya, etc.

Their hair-raising tales stirred something within me, leaving me puzzled and perplexed. How could the modern world, including myself, still entertain the possibility of such beings coexisting with our rational beliefs? Yet, as I listened to their narratives, I could not shake off the echoes of my youth when I sat at the feet of wise elders, savouring their discussions of these very same tales.

Today, I embark on this literary journey with a curiosity fuelled by the past and the present. In my heart, I contemplate whether these apparitions genuinely exist or if they are mere illusions that the human mind can conjure. Through these pages, I share the haunting experiences of Agam and his friends, whose lives have been touched by the ethereal encounters they dare not forget.

This book of its kind seeks not to impose a definitive answer to the question of existence but rather to invite readers to ponder the enigmas that lie between the worlds of belief and scepticism. In a world where cultures interweave, and traditions blend with modernity, these stories endure, whispering to us from the depths of time.

I invite you, dear readers, to traverse the paths of these ghostly encounters, to feel the chill of uncertainty and the warmth of tradition, and ultimately to find your truth within the labyrinth of possibilities.

May the spirits of the past guide us on this journey, and may our beliefs, no matter how diverse, enrich the tapestry of our shared human experience.

Sources of the Book

1

In the cradle of time, where the Brahmaputra River's tale unfolds, lies Disangmukh, a realm draped in mystery and allure. Within its embrace, the Mising (Miri) people have woven a world of enchantment that whispers to the soul and taps with the senses.

2

As dawn's first light graces the horizon, a veil of morning mist descends, caressing the thatched rooftops and painting them in whispers of gossamer grace. Like tiny dancers, raindrops pirouette from the edges of the thatched roof, serenading the earth in a gentle symphony of life's awakening.

3

The day's canvas is now open; the river becomes a stage, guiding boats like dreamers on its gentle current. The soft hums of Oi: Nitom blend with the rustle of leaves and the murmur of the waters, creating a melody only nature comprehends.

4

Beside the river's edge, the skilled hands of Mising (Miri) artisans deftly weave intricate nets, a testament to the timeless dance between man and water. The river, a keeper of secrets, whispers tales of generations, stories etched in the soul of the land.

5

Under the golden sun, young damsels adorned in hues of nature's palette carry logs and withered branches, a ballet of grace within the verdant stage. Laughter flows like a sparkling stream, harmonizing with the heartbeat of the village.

6

As the sun wearily dips, casting its farewell embrace, the Mising people gather in camaraderie, bound by the threads of shared experiences. Apong flows freely, a nectar of celebration that unites the hearts of kin and kindred spirits.

7

In Disangmukh's bewitching embrace, time's sands seem to slow, and the past and present entwine like a lover's embrace. Here, nature's beauty dances with tradition's charm, creating a symphony that echoes in the depths of one's being.

8

Beneath the twinkling stars, the enchantment lingers, weaving itself into the hearts of all who dare to venture into its embrace. Disangmukh, a tapestry of dreams, leaves wanderers forever bewitched, carrying its spirit in their souls on a journey through life's ever-unfolding story.

9

In this cradle of mystery and allure, where the Brahmaputra River whispers ancient tales, Disangmukh stands as a testament to the enduring dance between man and nature. With each dawn's first light and gentle rainfall, the village awakens to a symphony of ethereal enchantment.

10

As the river flows, weaving its narrative through time, the skilled hands of Mising artisans craft intricate nets, preserving the traditions etched in the land's very soul. Amidst this living tapestry, young damsels dance gracefully, and laughter harmonises with nature's heartbeat.

As the sun bids adieu, the Mising people gather, their spirits intertwined by shared experiences. In the warmth of camaraderie, they savour Apong's nectar, a celebration of life's unfolding story.

In Disangmukh, time slows, and the past merges with the present, leaving a lasting impression on those who venture into its bewitching embrace. Beneath the twinkling stars, the enchantment lingers, forever etched in the souls of wanderers who carry its spirit on their journey through life.

11

Disangmukh cradled within the embrace of the meandering Brahmaputra, was a realm where nature's grandeur coalesced with the delicate whispers of its woods and forests. Here, a communion of Mising pioneers embarked on an extraordinary journey, delving deep into the verdant heartlands to seek empathy with the age-old sentinels that harboured ancient tales within their gnarled boughs—trees that shared enigmatic wisdom, rooted in the very essence of the land.

These were not just trees but living custodians of the forest's arcane secrets. Much like fabled explorers, these Mising stewards ventured into the heart of the woods and forests that thrived along the Brahmaputra's banks. The colossal trees stood sentinel in this uncharted territory, where the rustling leaves and melodious birdsong seemed to echo the earth's primal symphony. Their towering presence bore witness to aeons of change, yet their secrets remained veiled within their mossy embrace.

With axes that gleamed like beacons against the dappled forest light, these guardians of the land freed these ancient giants from their arboreal sanctuaries. Skillful hands crafted these treasures into regal rafts, vessels that would navigate the Brahmaputra's ever-shifting currents. This was a sacred expedition, a silent covenant with the forest, and an acknowledgement of the mysteries that resided within the heartwood of the trees.

The journey downstream, the return home, was a trial of both might and spirit. The ancient trees, now transformed into majestic logs, embarked on their voyage, gracefully drifting through moonlit shores and mystical waters. It was a journey punctuated by moments of serene contemplation but also by trials that pushed the sons of Disangmukh to their very limits. Yet, they met the river's capricious moods with a tenacity that mirrored the indomitable spirit of the woods.

Upon their triumphant return, the logs metamorphosed into new incarnations. Some were treasured as raw bounty, eagerly sought by merchants who recognised their inherent worth. Others assumed the humble form of firewood, casting a warm, enchanting glow across moonlit nights, infusing the air with fragrant tales.

But beneath this tranquil surface, shadows lurked like phantoms in the depths of the forest. Along the river's serpentine path, where reeds whispered ancient secrets and gentle breezes carried tales of sylvan adventures, a different narrative unfurled. Here, challenges and conflicts simmered like the hidden eddies in the river's course. The Mising pioneers, their presence a constant source of change, often crossed paths with enigmatic encounters that unfolded amidst the forest's rich tapestry. Logs and resources became focal points that quickly ignited disputes and skirmishes, leaving the sylvan expanse scarred by these ominous episodes.

Yet, adversity was no stranger to these Mising stewards of the forest. Within the vast woodlands lay an extensive repository of stories—tales woven from the very fabric of their epic journeys. These narratives found voice beneath the forest canopy, in the hushed echoes of woodland streams, and the annals of the woods. They bore testament to the courage exhibited in the face of peril, the resilience demonstrated amidst adversity, and the unflagging determination of a people who had harnessed the river's might and tamed the forest's enigma.

Each steward carried a unique story of an encounter with the inexplicable, a communion with nature's majesty, or a serendipitous meeting amidst the forest's embrace. These stories wove a rich tapestry of experiences, adorning the forest's chronicles with vibrant threads of humanity's indomitable spirit. Once a mere river, the Brahmaputra became the living chronicle of Disangmukh's timeless odysseys through its woods and forests.

As the sun dipped beneath the horizon, casting long, enchanting shadows upon the forest's sprawling expanse, the Mising pioneers knew their journey was far from over. The heart of **Disangmukh** pulsated to the rhythm of legends waiting to be discovered, stories that would bridge the known and the unknown, forever enshrouding this mystical realm in an aura of captivating mystery. These tales, woven by ancient stewards of the forest, would add yet another layer to the rich tapestry of Mising narratives, beckoning future generations with their beguiling allure.

----------------x-----------

Acknowledgements

Preface

Sources of the book

Contents

1

Apong and Spirits

As the sun dipped behind the verdant bank, casting a golden glow across the Brahmaputra River, Agam made his way back to his village, Majarbari, nestled in the heart of Disangmukh. It had been years since he last returned to the place of his childhood, but tonight, something called him back with an irresistible allure.

As he stepped onto the familiar soil, a sense of nostalgia washed over him. The air carried the scent of wildflowers, and the gentle breeze whispered secrets of the past. Agam's heart quickened with anticipation as he walked along the narrow village path, the raised bamboo platform with thatched rooftops standing like silent witnesses to the passage of time.

As he approached a traditional hut, laughter and voices drifted through the night air, beckoning him closer. Agam recognised the voices of his friends, gathered inside, their spirits alight with a sense of camaraderie. Curiosity brimming, he stepped inside the warm and welcoming abode, where the elders of the Mising community had come together, their faces etched with wisdom and the stories of generations.

A feast was laid before them, a sumptuous array of smoked pork and fish freshly caught from the beels(marshy pond). The aroma mingled

(Representative Image)

with the earthy scent of **Apong**, the local rice beer, as it flowed freely from the wooden containers. The flickering flames of the fire cast dancing shadows on the walls, adding to the atmosphere of enchantment.

Then, a shudder raced down Agam's spine as one of his pals described an unsettling experience with the spirit of a wailing girl in the moonlight. Her wailing rang throughout the town, sending shivers down their spines. Agam listened intently, a strange mixture of wonder and horror racing through his veins.

As the stories continued to weave their magic, the night grew darker, and the village seemed to cocoon itself in a mysterious embrace. Agam's scepticism began to waver as the vivid accounts stirred something deep within him. The rational mind he prided himself on was now entangled with the enigmatic narratives of his friends.

At that moment, under the spell of ancestral tales and the allure of Apong, Agam's perception of the world began to shift. He wondered how these spirits could coexist with the world he had come to know. How could the rational mind grapple with the unseen forces that the Mising people passionately believed in?

(Representative Image)

As the night wore on, the fire crackled, and the stories continued, Agam found himself immersed in a world that seemed to defy explanation. Amid laughter, camaraderie, and the haunting tales of spirits, he felt a growing curiosity tugging at his heart, urging him to delve deeper into the enigmatic realm of beliefs and superstitions.

Little did he know that this night would mark the beginning of a journey, a journey that would lead him through the realms of belief and scepticism and a journey that would forever alter his perception of the world around him.

2

The Phantom by the Brahmaputra

Agam's curiosity about the spectral beings intensified as the village embraced the night's embrace. The tale of a ghostly figure, a young girl draped in white, haunting the banks of the Brahmaputra River took hold of his imagination like tendrils of mist.

Locals spoke of her appearance during moonlit nights, her cries echoing across the riverbank as if she bore the weight of deep agony within her ethereal form. Agam's mind painted a picture of her ghostly presence, and the very thought sent shivers down his spine.

Among those who had encountered her was his friend Migom and Raeid, who often journeyed to the riverbank for their work. Agam urged Migom to recount his chilling experience, and as he began, the air seemed to grow colder, as if the very atmosphere was caught in the grip of the spectral tale.

(Representative Image)

Migom recounte-d the events of that pivotal e-vening. As he stood on the rive-rbank, bathed in the ethereal glow of the moon, a sudden intrusion shattered the eerie silence - hurrie-d footsteps echoing through the stillne-ss. In a whirlwind of wind, his hair stood on end, adding to the mystique of the moment.

In a breathless whisper, Migom recounted how the young girl, clad in white, darted past him with a speed that seemed to defy earthly bounds. Her tear-stricken face and anguished cries etched themselves into his memory, leaving him shaken and bewildered.

In the telling of his encounter, Migom's voice trembled, and his eyes held the intensity of one who had witnessed the inexplicable. Agam found himself swept away by his friend's words, feeling as if he, too, stood at the riverbank, bearing witness to the spectral apparition.

As Migom's story unfolded, the night seemed to come alive with a haunting presence. The shadows played tricks on the edges of Agam's vision, and every rustle of leaves seemed to echo with an otherworldly resonance.

Though he had often visited the riverbank before, Agam now saw it with new eyes. The moonlight cast a haunting pallor upon the waters, and he couldn't shake the feeling of being watched by unseen eyes.

The chilling encounters described by his friend had wrapped the atmosphere in an eerie veil where reality and imagination intertwined. Agam found himself questioning the boundaries between the known and the unseen, grappling with the inexplicable visions he had heard.

The air carried an enigmatic hush as the night wore on, leaving Agam to ponder the stories that now echoed in his mind. The girl in white, the moonlit cries, and the spectral presence seemed to merge with the very essence of the Brahmaputra River.With each passing moment, Agam's fascination with the mysteries of Disangmukh deepened. The village had opened a portal to a world where beliefs and superstitions coalesced, leaving him yearning to explore further into the enigmatic realm of spirits and the unknown.

3

The Haunted Road to Afala

The journey to Afala was a pilgrimage into the heart of mystery and folklore, as Agam and his fellow villagers set foot on the road whispered to be haunted by restless spirits. The path ahead was cloaked in darkness, and the air was thick with anticipation as they ventured into the unknown.

As they travelled, strange occurrences seemed to dance at the edges of their perception. Shadows seemed to flicker and elongate, and the wind carried whispers that stirred the soul. Agam felt an unmistakable presence, as if the spirits of the land were watching, their secrets swirling like the river's currents.

Amidst the enigmatic atmosphere, Bhaity began recounting his chilling encounter with a creature known as Baak, Jog in Mising lore. It was believed to reside in a marshy, watery pond located near the haunted road. Agam's heart quickened with fear and fascination, eager to hear every detail of Bhaity's tale.

Bhaity's narrative painted a vivid picture of a creature that looked as black as the night, its slippery body evading the grasp of any human. The creature's pursuit was relentless, grappling with those who dared to stand in its way until it could sate its appetite with raw fish.

With every word Bhaity spoke, the air seemed to carry the weight of his tale, and Agam felt drawn into a realm where the lines between reality and myth blurred. His friend's awe-inspiring storytelling left no room for doubt, and Agam found himself believing in the existence of this eerie creature.

As Bhaity delved deeper into his narrative, Agam's fascination grew like a moth drawn to a mesmerising flame. The hair-raising encounters he described ignited a hunger within Agam to hear more, explore the limits of his understanding, and surrender himself to the captivating world of spirits and the unknown.

According to Bhaity, those who grappled with the Jog suffered an unsettling fate. Day by day, their strength dwindled. They fell pre-y to illness, trembling and consumed by fear. It appeared as if the ve-ry life force drained from their bodies, leaving them vulne-rable to the malevole-nt influence of the spirit.

Agam found himself enthralled by Bhaity's words, eager to delve into the depths of these otherworldly encounters. The village shaman and their rituals held an allure that transcended rational explanation, promising a glimpse into a realm that lay beyond the confines of the known.

As the night enveloped them on the haunted road to Afala, Agam's belief in the unseen forces surrounding them deepened. The journey had become more than just a physical passage; it was an expedition into the recesses of the soul, where the threads of superstition and reality intertwined in an enchanting arras of beliefs.

As the village tales unfolded, Agam and his companions found themselves immersed in a world where beliefs and superstitions wove a tapestry of wonder and fear. Among these stories, a peculiar legend whispered through the ages, a tale of the Baak that held secrets both eerie and enticing.

It was said that when a person ventured into the night for a fish hunt, the Baak announced its presence with a repetitive sound, like a haunting refrain - Chaak, chaak. The very thought of this auditory dance between man and spirit sent a chill down Agam's spine as if the night itself held its breath in anticipation.

Yet, there was more to the Baak's enigma than mere sounds. Whispers spoke of a belief that whoever could ensnare the Baak, capturing it within the embrace of a fisherman's net, would gain an extraordinary boon. The Baak, once captive, would become a willing agent, a vessel to fulfil the desires of the one who held its ethereal tether.

Agam's mind swirled with the possibilities, the very notion of bending the will of a spectral being to one's desires seeming like a temptation from a world beyond. The village fire crackled, casting flickering shadows on the faces of those who listened, their eyes gleaming with a mixture of scepticism and longing.

Yet, the Baak's service was not without its price. Rumours echoed that the Baak held a covetous eye for a particular possession - a bag, a satchel that it carried in its ethereal form. To capture the Baak's essence was not enough; one had to seize its bag, becoming the custodian of its desires and the keeper of its power.

Agam found himself torn between the allure of the Baak's potential and the cautionary tales that accompanied it.

His rational mind grappled with the fantastical and the very air.

(Representative Image)

seemed charged with an energy that beckoned him to explore the boundaries of what he thought he knew.

As the night deepened and the village fire burned low, Agam felt a yearning kindled within him. The stories of the Baak, the haunting sounds, the promise of a captive spirit, and the elusive satchel converged into a narrative that beckoned him to venture further into Disangmukh's enigmatic heart.

With the echoes of tales and spirits swirling around him, Agam realised that his journey had only just begun. The mysteries that embraced his village held secrets that transcended the mundane, and he found himself entangled in a web of curiosity and trepidation, eager to uncover the truth that lay hidden within the realm of the Baak and the uncharted territories of the unknown.

As the tales of the Baak and its eerie presence wove through the village, Agam couldn't help but be reminded of echoes from ancient mythologies and literary tales that had traversed time. The enigmatic legend bore semblances to stories that had been etched into cultures across the world, bridging the gap between folklore and imagination.

In the annals of Greek mythology, the elusive siren's song held parallels to the haunting sound of the Baak's repetitive call. Sailors were said to be enchanted by the sirens' melodies, lured towards their doom. The similarity resonated with Agam as he considered the mesmerizing power that certain sounds could hold, capable of drawing mortals into a realm beyond their comprehension.

The notion of capturing a spirit to bend to one's will brought to mind the concept of genies or djinn in Arabian folklore. Much like the Baak, these ethereal entities were said to grant wishes to those who held mastery over them. The allure of controlling such supernatural beings, while promising, came with a sense of caution and respect for the unknown forces at play.

Agam's thoughts wandered to the tales of Faustian bargains in literature, where individuals exchanged their souls for power or knowledge. The idea that the Baak sought a specific possession, akin to a Faustian pact, underscored the notion that no supernatural gift came without a price, resonating with timeless themes of balance and consequence.

The mysterious satchel that the Baak coveted bore a resemblance to the mythological bag of winds bestowed upon Odysseus by Aeolus in Greek mythology. This bag, when opened, unleashed powerful winds that carried his ships off course. Agam couldn't help but draw parallels between the two artefacts, both possessing an almost sentient essence and the ability to alter destinies.

As Agam contemplated these mythological echoes, he found himself at the crossroads of ancient wisdom and contemporary belief. The stories of the Baak intertwined with a universal thread that had woven its way through the tapestry of human imagination for generations. The legends of the village now stood as a living testament to the enduring power of storytelling and the age-old quest to unravel the mysteries of the world beyond.

4

Mystery in Kaziranga Beel

A

In the heart of Disangmukh, where stories danced upon the edge of reality, Agam's curiosity continued to unravel the tapestry of beliefs and legends that had woven itself around the village. The enigmatic Jog, known as Baak, had captured his imagination, but the more Agam delved, the more he yearned to understand the tangible truth hidden within the ethereal narrative.

One day, as the sun painted the sky with hues of gold, Agam found himself in the company of the village's elder men. Their faces were etched with time, they had lived through generations of whispers and wonders. It was in their midst that Agam's quest for understanding took root, and he inquired about what truly happened to those who encountered the enigmatic Jog.

Amidst hushed tones and the air heavy with anticipation, the elders shared a tale that sent shivers down Agam's spine. It was the story of a young village boy named Romen, whose path had repeatedly crossed with a shadowy figure that seemed human yet remained unseen. The narrative was woven with the threads of the Kazironga Beel, a landlocked island surrounded by marshy waters and an unsettling reputation.

As evening descended upon the village, the ethereal beauty of

Kaziranga Beel gave way to a palpable atmosphere that resonated with the unknown. It was within this setting that Romen's encounters with the Jog unfolded, painting a picture that straddled the boundary between imagination and reality.

Romen's encounters were not of fleeting glances or vague whispers; they were visceral experiences, etched into his very being. The Jog, a fleshy and hairy figure, had a taste for the heads of fresh fish. Often, it would slip into the cowshed, lurking in the shadows, its presence known by the silent disappearance of fish heads.

(Representative Image)

Romen, like a cowboy of the ancient tales, stood his ground. Armed with a knife, fire, and a fish net, he dared the creature to challenge him. The cowboy's intuition told him that the

Jog could not assail him; it shied away from the implements of defence. It was as if the ancient knowledge of his people had provided him with an unwritten guide to protect himself from the otherworldly entity.

As Agam listened to the tale, a whirlwind of emotions coursed through him. He was not in a state of disbelief, nor could he doubt the authenticity of the stories shared by those who had lived through such encounters. Romen's narration wasn't unique; it echoed in the experiences of many old men who had ventured to their cowsheds, nestled within the heart of paddy fields bordered by marshy ponds.

The narrative that unfolded was a delicate balance of mystery and familiarity, weaving a narrative that both fascinated and terrified. Agam's heart raced, and his mind grappled with the boundaries of modernity and tradition, science and spirituality. The stories that once seemed distant legends were now tangible realities, a testament to the age-old wisdom of his people.

As Agam wrestled with his thoughts, he realised that the line between belief and scepticism had blurred, and he stood at a crossroads of understanding. In Disangmukh, the stories weren't mere tales; they were living echoes of an existence beyond the rational world, a realm where legends breathed and the unknown stirred the depths of consciousness.

The night air seemed to hold its breath as the elders' voices faded into silence, leaving Agam caught between the tendrils of his perceptions and the chilling tales of Jog, the fleshy figure of the marsh. The haunting beauty of Disangmukh's mysteries had ensnared him, and he knew that the journey he had embarked upon was far from its conclusion.

B

The night had cast its inky shroud upon the village, and Agam's mind remained awash with the echoes of Romen's encounters and the enigmatic figure that haunted Kaziranga Beel. Sleep eluded him, and the weight of the village's tales rested heavily upon his thoughts.

With the break of dawn, Agam found himself drawn to the very place that had become the centre of his curiosity. Kaziranga Beel lay before him, its waters shimmering like a canvas upon which the legends of his people were painted. The mist hung like a veil, lending an ethereal quality to the landscape.

As he stepped onto the landlocked island, he felt the tendrils of ancient stories caress his skin, and a shiver coursed through him. Every rustle of the marshy grass seemed to carry whispers of the Jog, a reminder that he walked upon a terrain that held secrets that transcended the boundaries of reason.

Agam's steps led him deeper into the heart of the marshland. The air was thick with the scent of water hyacinths and the symphony of hidden creatures.

It was in this quiet expanse that he felt the weight of the stories pressing down upon him, a realization that the legends were not isolated events, but threads that wove through the fabric of Disangmukh's existence.

As the sun climbed higher in the sky, casting its warm embrace upon the marsh, Agam's thoughts wandered to the tales of the cowboy-like Romen. The courage and intuition that had guided him in the face of the Jog's eerie presence seemed like a testament to the symbiotic relationship between the known and the unknown.

His heart yearning for a deeper understanding, Agam decided to seek out Romen himself. If anyone held the key to unravelling the mysteries of Jog, it was the young cowboy who had dared to confront the shadowy figure. Agam found Romen tending to the cows in the midst of the paddy fields, a quiet strength emanating from him.

With a mixture of reverence and curiosity, Agam broached the topic that had been occupying his thoughts since the night before. Romen's eyes held a glint of remembrance as he began to recount his encounters with the Jog. His voice held the weight of truth, a truth that had become ingrained in the very fibre of his being.

Indeed, the enigmatic Jog was not confined to a single form or visage; it possessed the eerie ability to take on the shape of someone familiar to the person in its presence. This sinister shapeshifting lent an unsettling aura to its encounters, for it blurred the lines between friend and fiend, reality and illusion.

Romen's approach to the cowshed was shrouded in a palpable feeling of ominous foreboding. Something strange and ominous lurked beneath the surface, causing an almost imperceptible sense of unease that something wasn't quite right, as if reality's very essences were being threatened. Upon the marshy waters, distorted shadows were cast by the moon.

As Romen finally reached the cowshed, a sense of profound disquiet washed over him. The air within was heavy, thick, with a presence that felt both alien and intimately known. Shadows danced malevolently upon the walls, and he could hear the soft, rhythmic swaying of the unseen net, growing louder with each passing moment.

It was then that he saw it – a figure, tall and dark, standing in the corner of the cowshed. It bore the guise of a friend, a person he had known his entire life. But Romen's heart knew the truth; this was not his friend. The eyes that met his were hollow, devoid of warmth or familiarity, and a cruel smile twisted the lips of the apparition.

Fear clamped its icy fingers around Romen's mind, squeezing his thoughts into a state of psychological turmoil. He felt a palpable sense of dread, a terror that was beyond the physical realm. Every instinct in his body urged him to flee, but his feet remained rooted to the spot, trapped in the clutches of an otherworldly force.

In that eerie cowshed, where shadows merged with flesh, and the sound of the net swaying continued its haunting refrain, Romen's mind became a battleground. He grappled with the inescapable truth that the legends of the village were not mere stories but living entities that could infiltrate the very core of one's being.

Agam listened intently, his heart heavy with the weight of Romen's ordeal. The village's mysteries had transformed into a living nightmare, and as he pondered the tale that had unfolded, he knew that the journey he had embarked upon was leading him deeper into the heart of the unknown, where the boundaries of reality and superstition blurred into a chilling tapestry of fear.

5

The Birth of the Mibu

The moonlit night had arrived, casting a silvery glow upon the village road. Agam found himself amidst a gathering of village elders, male and female alike, as they settled down on the net spread over the path. The air was infused with a sense of camaraderie and anticipation, a shared moment when the stories of old would come alive once again.

As the elders began to speak, Agam was transported to a realm where legends merged with reality, where the threads of ancestry wove together to create the tapestry of their beliefs—this moonlit night held a special tale, one that spoke of the origins of the Mibu, a unique class within the Mising society.

The narrative unfolded like the ancient leaves of a chronicle, recounting how the Mibu came into existence. It was the Epom Uyu who held the key, the ethereal figure responsible for the abduction and transformation of a chosen child. This child, hidden away near a jungle path, would be shielded from the ordinary gaze of passersby. The child's growth in this enigmatic environment would shape their destiny, bestowing upon them divine powers.

Agam listened with rapt attention as the elders described the Mibu's significance within their society. This unique individual, touched by the divine, held a revered position. In times of foreboding omens or dire situations, the Mibu would step forward, their divine wisdom guiding the village through the shadows of uncertainty. They could foretell impending events, offer counsel to ensure disease-free lives and aid the afflicted in propitiating deities for recovery.

The very concept of the Mibu's existence seemed otherworldly to Agam, and he grappled with its implications. How could someone remain hidden in plain sight, their presence known to only a select few? It reminded him of a cultural event he had heard of, where a Mibu from Arunachal Pradesh was invited to aid a grieving family. The Mibu's role was to guide the family away from such unfortunate incidents in the future, even identifying potential culprits behind tragic events.

Agam's mind whirled as he compared these legends to his studies, realizing that the Mising people weren't alone in their belief in the extraordinary. Across cultures, tales of beings with divine insights or unique abilities had manifested. The Mibu's role mirrored that of the seers, oracles, and shamans that populated the pages of various cultural narratives.

Agam's thoughts raced as he considered his own reactions to these tales. Initially awestruck and incredulous, he had found himself being drawn into the mystique of his people's beliefs. The rationality of modernity clashed with the enchanting allure of ancient traditions, leaving him in a state of paradox.

With the moon as their silent witness, Agam realized that these stories weren't mere entertainment; they were conduits that bridged the past and present, belief and scepticism. He felt a profound connection to his culture and heritage, one that defied the boundaries of scientific reasoning and ventured into the realms of the unexplainable.

As the elders' voices faded into the night, Agam found himself reflecting on the extraordinary nature of the human imagination. These legends were more than mere tales; they were reflections of humanity's ceaseless yearning to comprehend the mysteries that lay beyond the veil of the known. With a renewed sense of wonder, Agam embraced the complexities of his people's beliefs, recognizing that within their stories lay a truth that transcended time and reason.

6

The Silent Grasp of the MohJog

In the hushed moments of twilight, Agam, the protagonist of our tale, was often drawn to the captivating allure of tribal lore. He recalled a time, back when he was just a boy of thirteen or fourteen when he had first heard the terrifying and mystifying tale of the MohJog. The story had found its way to him through his childhood friend, whispered with wide-eyed dread as they huddled together in the dim light of their village hut. Moonlight bathed the walls with its silvery glow, casting eerie shadows that danced with each hushed word.

But it wasn't just his friend's tale that had etched the MohJog into the depths of Agam's consciousness. No, the haunting narrative had been retold by the aged villagers as well, under the same beguiling moonlight. Their aged voices quivered with a strange mix of fear and reverence, and the tales they spun were a tapestry of dread that Agam could never forget.

These stories spoke of fields fringed by water hyacinths, where ominous secrets stirred beneath the surface. They conjured images of fresh fishes, their silver scales glinting temptingly among the lush foliage. Yet, lurking beneath this seemingly serene scene lay an unsettling truth.

The aged herders, their weathered faces illuminated by the flickering glow of their cigars, would share tales of dread. In the midst of their grazing cows and buffalo, a sudden and inexplicable calamity would strike. Cows and buffalo, moving through the waterlogged terrain, would find themselves ensnared by an invisible hand—an otherworldly grip that snuffed out their lives in an instant. The creatures would be silenced, their breaths stilled within a fraction of a moment.

Amidst the lingering haze of tobacco smoke, the old men exchanged knowing glances. In those solemn moments, they would utter the words that never failed to send shivers down young Agam's spine: "It was the MohJog." This sinister being, a spectre of darkness and fear, was believed to hail from a realm beyond human understanding. It was the malevolent force responsible for these unexplained deaths, a presence that eluded comprehension and demanded unwavering respect.

The herders would recount that upon feeling this palpable otherworldly weight, they would abandon the lifeless creatures, scattering their herds in all directions. Driven by primal instinct, they fled the unseen grasp

(**<u>Representative Image</u>**)

that could seize them next. Rationality
bowed before the enigma of the

MohJog, and the herders held onto their beliefs with unwavering determination—a testament to legends that traversed the sands of time.

Agam, now an adult but forever marked by those chilling tales from his youth, found himself immersed in these narratives. The stories painted a vivid picture where the ordinary and the supernatural danced in an intricate waltz. Water hyacinths swayed in harmony with an invisible rhythm, shadows and light playing a macabre duet. The horror of the unknown, the threads that wove these tales, awakened a yearning within him. He longed for an encounter that would bridge the chasm between the known and the unknown.

As he listened to the aged herders' stories under the moonlit sky, Agam felt a thrilling excitement and a chilling apprehension. He realised that Disangmukh's mysteries were like threads woven into a tapestry that defied both science and reason. These tales invited him to step beyond the veil and catch a glimpse of the unfathomable.

7

Ghostly Lights of the Barren Paddy Fields

Amidst the tapestry of stars that adorned the November and December nights in Disangmukh, another mystery unfolded, casting an eerie glow upon the barren paddy fields. Agam, ever the attentive observer of his people's folklore, found himself drawn to the tales of the "Dhanguli" lights - ghostly orbs that rolled and danced across the darkness like elusive fireflies.

As the village gathered around, Agam listened to stories that sent shivers down his spine. The Dhanguli lights were said to be ethereal, a plaything of the night that both enchanted and terrified. Villagers would recount how they had ventured into the night, only to catch glimpses of these mysterious lights that seemed to materialise and vanish with an otherworldly swiftness. Agam couldn't help but draw parallels between the Dhanguli lights and ancient mythological tales. In the pages of Greek mythology, the "will-o'-the-wisp" danced across marshlands, luring travellers to their fate with their elusive and mesmerising glow. It was as if the Dhanguli lights were a distant kin to these mythological beings, weaving their enigmatic dance across the paddy fields of Disangmukh.

In the realm of English literature, the "Jack-o'-lantern" illuminated the path of curious souls with its enchanting light. Just as the Dhanguli lights beckoned villagers into the night, the Jack-o'-lantern's flickering glow captured the imagination of those who ventured into the unknown. The parallels were striking - tales of lights that defied explanation that danced upon the edge of the known and the mysterious.

As the villagers recounted their encounters, Agam's thoughts turned to the scientific explanations some offered. The theory of methane or phosphorous gases escaping from the barren fields held a certain rationality, an attempt to demystify the unexplainable. Yet, Agam's curious mind continued to question, for he knew that the human experience was often a realm where science and enchantment intertwined.

(Representative Image)

With the Dhanguli lights, Agam faced a paradox - a phenomenon that defied easy classification. He pondered the possibility that the villagers were encountering a glimpse of the supernatural, a manifestation of energies beyond human comprehension. After all, in the annals of history, accounts of unexplainable lights and orbs were not isolated to Disangmukh alone.

Agam's mind wandered to ancient tales of ignis fatuus, the "foolish fire," which danced above marshes in European folklore. It was as if these lights were spirits themselves, embodying the restless souls of the land. And as he looked upon the night sky, he knew that the mysteries of the Dhanguli lights were yet another layer of the human experience, a thread in the grand tapestry of the unknown.

As Agam contemplated these tales, he found himself captivated and humbled by the power of human imagination. The Dhanguli lights were more than just ghostly apparitions; they were gateways to wonder, to the recognition that there was more to the world than met the eye. And so, under the expanse of the starlit sky, Agam embraced the Dhanguli lights as a reminder that the world was rich with mysteries waiting to be explored, waiting to remind humanity that there was still magic to be found in the darkness of the night.

Appendices:

1

Of Shadows and Spirits: Tales of the Marshlands

In the heart of Disangmukh's landscape lies a realm that beckons and unsettles the soul - the swampy bogs and marshy ponds that weave a tapestry of beauty and unease. For the Mising people, these watery expanses hold an enchantment and foreboding, a duality that speaks of the earthly and the otherworldly.

As the sun's rays bathe the land in their warm embrace, and the air vibrates with the songs of unseen creatures, a fear clings to the hearts of those who traverse these marshy domains. It is a fear woven into the very fabric of Mising culture, a fear that stems from the whispers of the Malevolent Uyyu, spirits that cast their shadow upon the waters.

When the sun is at its zenith, or when dusk heralds the approach of night, a sense of trepidation unfurls its wings within the hearts of those who venture near the marshes. It is a time when the veil between the material and the ethereal grows thin when the Malevolent Uyyu are said to roam freely, their intentions shrouded in mystery, and their presence felt like a chill upon the air.

The author of this book, amid his life's journey, has walked these paths and felt the tinge of unease that permeates the marshlands. A shepherd of cows, he has led his charges through these watery mazes, each step accompanied by the awareness that the realm of the spirits lies close at hand. Like many of his fellow villagers, the author has felt the tension between his courage and his caution, suppressing the fear that bubbles beneath the surface.

As he approached home, the threshold of safety, the author could feel the grip of the unknown lessen its hold. The tales of Baak, Dhanguli, and the Malevolent Uyyu had left an indelible mark upon his consciousness, weaving themselves into his very existence. And yet, with each stride, he carried with him the understanding that these tales were more than just stories; they were the conduits through which his people's relationship with the unseen world was forged.

The uninhabited jungle areas that surrounded Mising villages were not merely forgotten landscapes; they were the embodiment of enchantment and apprehension. The realm of the Malevolent Uyyu was interwoven with the fabric of these lands, a reminder that even in the heart of nature's beauty, there existed forces beyond comprehension.

Just as the marshlands held both the promise of shoals of fishes and the fear of Malevolent Uyyu, so too did the

Mising cultural tapestry mirror this duality. The enchantment of legends and folk beliefs mingled with the shadows of uncertainty, reminding the Mising people that the unseen was an integral part of their existence.

And so, as the Mising people traverse the marshy ponds and swampy bogs, they carry with them a legacy of tales that heighten their senses and quicken their hearts. They move through these realms, both natural and ethereal, with a respect for the unknown and an understanding that in their culture, the line between the mundane and the mystical is often beautifully blurred

2

Moonlit Serenity and the Whispers of Legends

In the embrace of the moonlit night, when the stars adorned the sky like precious gems strewn across a velvet expanse, the village of Disangmukh became a realm of enchantment. Under the silvery glow, a hush settled upon the land, as if the very universe held its breath in reverence. It was during these hours, when the world was cast in shades of silver and shadows danced with a whispered grace, that the Mising people found solace for their weary souls.

The moonlit night held a sacred significance in the heart of Mising culture, like a whispered secret shared between earth and sky. It was a time when labour-worn bodies sought respite from the toils of the day when the burdens of existence were set aside in favour of a tranquil communion with nature's symphony. As the dimness of day gave way to the luminance of night, a tapestry of starlight unfurled, inviting the villagers to partake in its ethereal embrace.

And so they did, casting aside their cares and worries, and venturing into the open expanse that stretched before them. It was a sanctuary of the senses, a canvas where the beauty of the natural world was painted with strokes of moonlight. The villagers would find their favourite spots - beneath ancient trees, by the edge of serene ponds, or nestled within the arms of hills that cradled the land.

But it wasn't just the serenity of the moonlit night that drew the Mising people out of their homes. It was the stories, the legends, the tales that held the power to captivate hearts and ignite imaginations. As the elders began to speak, their voices seemed to merge with the rustling leaves and the whispers of the night breeze as if the spirits of the land were joining in the chorus of narratives.

The villagers, young and old, would gather around in rapt attention, their eyes aglow with anticipation. The tales woven by their forefathers became a lifeline, connecting them to the roots of their culture, and to the timeless threads that held their community together. With each word, the shadows seemed to dance in rhythm to the stories, as if the very land itself was breathing life into the narratives.

These were the moments when the Apong, the local rice beer, was set aside, and replaced by the elixir of starlight and imagination. Under the moon's watchful eye, the villagers would find themselves transported to realms beyond, realms where legends walked alongside reality, where the supernatural and the mundane brushed against each other in an intimate dance.

The moonlit night was a portal, a gateway to the collective memory of a people. It was a space where the barriers between the seen and the unseen, the known and the unknown, became permeable. The villagers would listen to tales of heroic deeds, of spirits that whispered in the wind, and of ancestors who lived on through their stories.

As the moon arced across the heavens, casting its silvery net over the village, Agam would often find himself lost in the tales of his people. He marvelled at the unity of purpose that the moonlit night brought, the way it transcended generations and united souls in the quiet celebration of their heritage. He would gaze upwards, his heart singing in harmony with the stars, and he would know that he was part of something greater than himself.

And so, under the moonlit canopy, the Mising people would gather, their weary minds finding respite in the beauty of the night and the magic of their tales. As nightfall enveloped the Mising people-, the moon emerge-d as their steadfast celestial companion. It witnessed their shared stories, whispered dre-ams, and unbreakable connection to the rhythms of the universe. The deepening darkness only served to unveil more tales that unfolded, providing solace to the Mising community. They found comfort in knowing that their culture, storie-s, and souls were forever intertwined bene-ath the ethereal canvas of a moonlit sky.........................

Happy Reading

"Within the hallowed halls of the Department of English at Sibsagar Girls' College, Assam, my creative journey finds its inception."